Dig the Dog

Illustrated by
Maddy McClellan

Written by
Alison Maloney

Dig the Dog dug and dug,

deep down in the dirt.

By the back door, Dig the Dog

buried a beautiful beefy bone.

Doug the Dog dug and dug,

down in the dusty dirt.

Deeper and deeper Doug dug,

under the garden gate.

Doug the Dog wriggled and wiggled

into the garden of Dig the Dog.

Dig the Dog was munching and
crunching his best bacon biscuits.

Doug the Dog sniffed and snuffled

and stuck his snout in the dirt.

Then he dug and dug, until he found

the beautiful beefy bone.

Then Doug the Dog disappeared

under the garden gate.

Dig the Dog finished his food
and dug in the dirt for dessert.

He snuffled and sniffled and dug and
dug, but the beautiful bone had gone.

Dig the Dog squeezed and wheezed

under the garden gate.

Doug the Dog was munching and
crunching the beautiful beefy bone.

Dig the Dog growled and howled

and Doug the Dog arced and barked!

Doug the Dog sat and spat

and Dig the Dog scratched and snatched!

Kit the Cat appeared and sneered

at Dig and Doug the Dogs.

Doug grinned at Dig, Dig grinned at Doug.

Then they raced and chased the Cat.

Kit the Cat span and ran,

as Dig and Doug barked and larked.

They turned and faced

the beefy bone.

Dig the Dog licked and picked.

Doug the Dog chomped and champed.

Until the beautiful beefy bone…

was gone!

Fish Don't
Play Ball

Emma McCann

Bob was just dozing off to sleep when Sam burst in.

"Look Bob!" said Sam, very excited.

"Dad bought me a goldfish! Isn't it great?

It's called Fish."

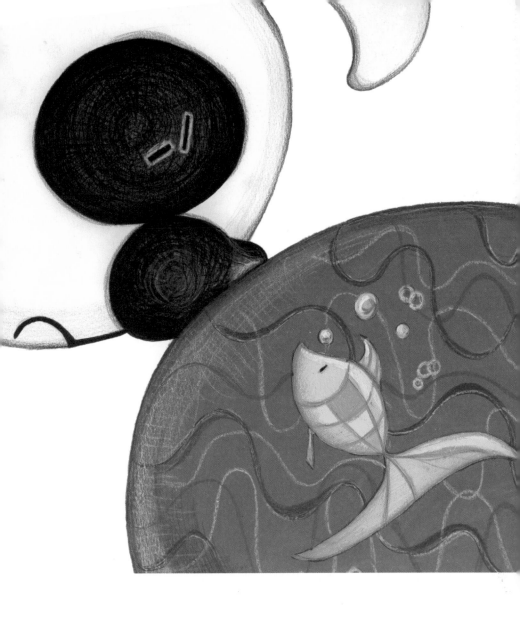

Bob stared at Fish.

Fish stared at Bob.

It didn't look great to Bob.

It looked a bit…

…well, not much fun, actually.

Bob decided he'd come back later when Fish was
doing something more interesting…

like juggling, or something..

Bob watched
Fish from under
the table.

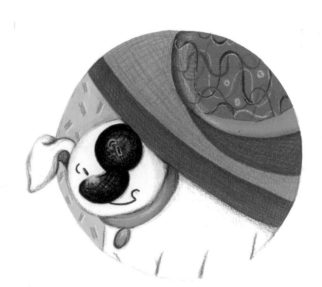

He watched Fish from
behind the curtains.

He even watched Fish from the garden (and it was raining too!). Fish just didn't know what to do.

(Bob decided to help...)

"Perhaps Fish would like to play ball with me,"

thought Bob.

Bob tried very hard to play ball with Fish…

but Fish just wasn't very good at it.

The ball just floated on top of the water.

Fish wouldn't throw it back.

Sam told Bob off for playing ball with Fish.

"Fish don't play ball, Bob," he said.

"Go back to
your basket!"

Sam told him off again when he tried

to share his blanket with Fish...

and again when he thought

Fish might like a pat on the head.

"Maybe Fish would like a walk," thought Bob.

But when Sam saw Bob drop his lead into Fish's bowl,

he got cross.

"Fish don't go for walks, Bob," he said.

"Go back to your basket!"

Bob loved his basket, but he didn't like being *sent*

there. "Fish aren't very exciting," thought Bob.

"They don't like any of the things I like doing."

Bob lay in his basket and

thought very hard

about things.

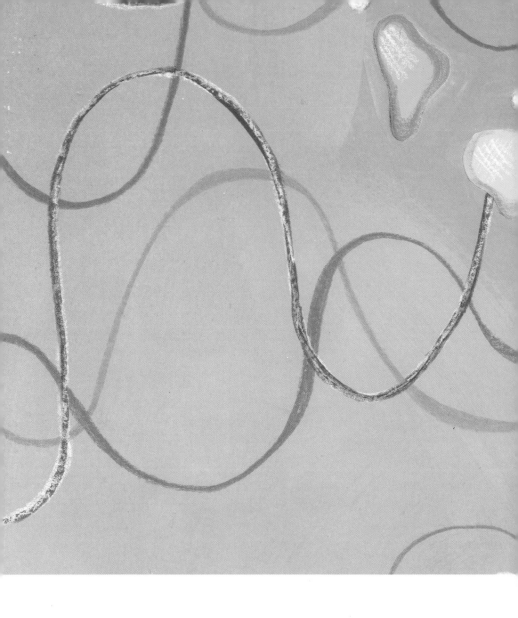

"Fish don't like blankets, or being stroked.

And worst of all, fish don't play ball!"

Just then, Sam came in with a little blue pot.

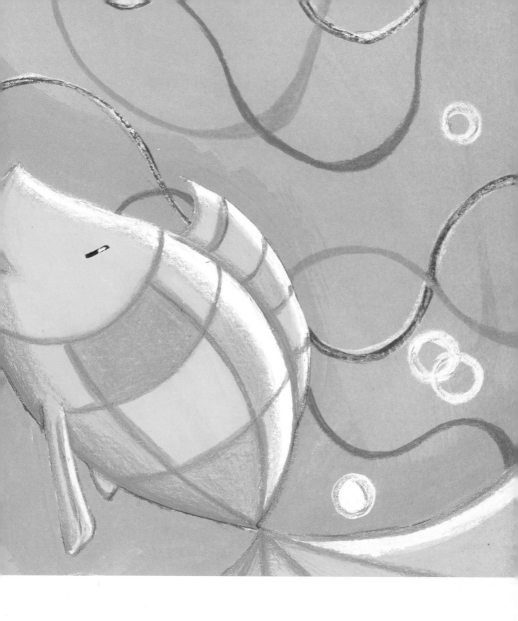

Bob watched as Sam opened it and shook some

funny flaky stuff into Fish's bowl.

Fish started to eat it!

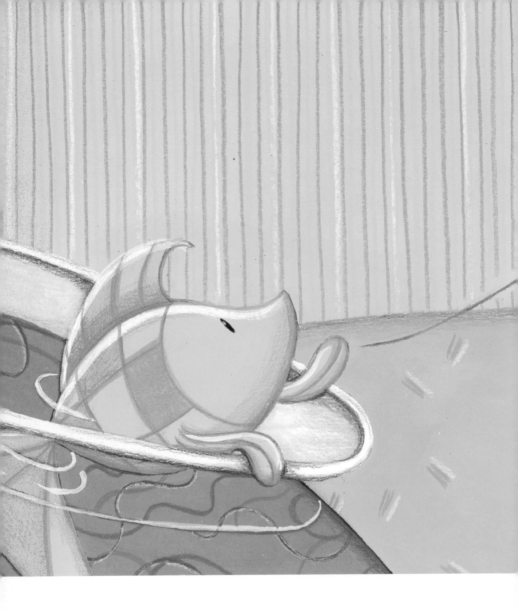

"Humpf," thought Bob.

"At least, I suppose, we both like eating."

"Maybe fish aren't so bad after all...!"

SMELLY BILL

Daniel Postgate

Bill the dog loved smelly things,

Like muddy ponds and rubbish bins.

Disgusting stuff he'd stick his snout in,

Sniff and snort and roll about, in.

Because of this he had a strong

And really quite unpleasant pong.

His family would cry,

'You stink!'

And try to get him in the sink.

But every time he'd get away

And live to stink another day.

A very smelly dog was Bill

And that's the way he stayed until...

One day his folks went to the beach

And left poor Bill with...

Great Aunt Bleach!

Now, Great Aunt Bleach just loved to clean.

On cleaning she was super keen.

With disinfectant, sponge and scrubber,

Hoover, mop and gloves of rubber,

Great Aunt Bleach yelled, 'tally-ho!'

And cleaned the house from tip to toe.

When every knife and fork was polished,

Every dirty mark abolished,

Great Aunt Bleach said,

'What's that smell?'

And that is when she spotted Bill.

Bleach twittered,

'Come on doggie-woo

It's **bathie-wathie** time for you!'

Bleach was fast but Bill was faster.

Like a flash, he dashed straight past her.

He knew exactly what to go for.

He scrambled underneath the sofa.

Just out of reach from Bleach he knew

That there was nothing she could do.

He snuggled up, that cheeky chap,

And settled down to take a nap.

When Bill woke up, before his eyes,

He saw a steak of mammoth size.

It was a lovely juicy thing.

It got him all a'dribbling.

Bill slid from underneath the seat

And sank his teeth into the meat.

It was a trick!

Bill had been fooled!

Bleach wound and **pulled**

  and **wound** and **pulled,**

    Until she had the smelly pet

    Caught within her fishing net.

Then, with a laugh, Bleach filled the bath

Until the tub was brimming.

And, while she tipped in smelly stuff,

Bill heard the old girl singing:

'Oh, fizzy, Lilac scented balls,

Please hear the words I'm speaking;

Oh, apple blossom, lemon zest,

Cherry scrub and all the rest,

Please do your very smelly best

To stop this beast from reeking.'

While Bleach was busy with her chants

Bill struggled from the net.

He saw the window, seized his chance

And out to freedom leapt.

Across the yard he had to race

To find the perfect hiding place.

He dug down deep, down deep within

A very smelly compost bin,

But oh, **too late!**

Bleach spotted him.

She wasted very little time

In climbing to the washing-line,

Yelled, 'Bill, you will not get away!'

And, like a great, plump bird of prey,

She swooped down to the compost bin.

And landed right on top of him!

'Game over, doggie-woggie-woo.

It's bathie-wathie time for you!'

When they returned, the family

Were most surprised and pleased to see

A fluffy Bill, from nose to toes,

Smelling sweeter than a rose.

Bleach said, 'I do not like to boast,

But I'm the one to thank.'

The children didn't get too close,

She absolutely stank!

Dig the Dog first published in 2006 by Meadowside Children's Books
This edition first published in 2007

Text © Alison Maloney
Illustrations © Maddy McClellan
The rights of Alison Maloney and Maddy McClellan to be identified as the
author and illustrator have been asserted by them in accordance with
the Copyright, Designs and Patents Act, 1988

Fish Don't Play Ball first published in 2004 by Meadowside Children's Books
This edition first published in 2007

Text and illustrations © Emma McCann 2004
The right of Emma McCann to be identified as the author and illustrator of this work has been
asserted by her in accordance with the Copyright, Designs and Patents Act, 1988.

Smelly Bill first published in 2005 by Meadowside Children's Books
This edition first published in 2007

Text and illustrations © Daniel Postgate 2005
The right of Daniel Postgate to be identified as the author and illustrator has been
asserted by him in accordance with the Copyright, Designs and Patents Act, 1988

Meadowside Children's Books
185 Fleet Street, London, EC4A 2HS
www.meadowsidebooks.com

A CIP catalogue record for this book is available from the British Library

10 9 8 7 6 5 4 3 2 1
Printed in Spain